W9-AXK-844

the
John Hancock
Club

ALSO BY LOUISE BORDEN

The Little Ships: The Heroic Rescue at Dunkirk in World War II

Good-Bye, Charles Lindbergh: Based on a True Story

Good Luck, Mrs. K.!

Sleds on Boston Common: A Story from the American Revolution

Fly High! The Story of Bessie Coleman

The Day Eddie Met the Author

America Is . . .

Touching the Sky: The Flying Adventures of Wilbur and Orville Wright

Sea Clocks: The Story of Longitude

The A+ Custodian

The Greatest Skating Race: A World War II Story from the Netherlands

The Last Day of School

Margaret K. McElderry Books

To
M. Kay Kroeger,

Johanna Hurwitz,
and
Terri Pytlik

Huzzah! to Sonia Chaghatzbanian

Huzzah! to Adam Gustavson

Huzzah! Huzzah! and many thanks
to my wonderful editor, Sarah Sevier
—L. B.

For Barb and Dan
—A. G.

the
John
Hancock
Club

written by
Louise Borden

illustrated by
Adam Gustavson

Margaret K. McElderry Books
New York London Toronto Sydney

*W*hen Hillside Elementary School began in late August,
the third graders in Mrs. Tovani's class
knew that *finally*
they would learn how to write their names,
homework,
and spelling words
in cursive handwriting.

Most of the students in Room 121 couldn't *wait* to get started.
They thought writing with fancy loops and swirls
would be much more fun than plain old printing.

But not Sean McFerrin.

School was already hard enough for Sean
without having to learn to write
in a new way . . .
and he worried that third grade
was going to take a lot more thinking
than second grade had.

Every morning,
Sean and the other third graders in Room 121
hurried up thirty-two wide stairs
and down a long hall to their classroom.

As the first weeks of September slipped by,
there were a dozen things
going on in Mrs. Tovani's room,
and the class hadn't even begun
to work on handwriting yet.

Sean loved studying the shapes of clouds . . .
making a map of America with the fifty states . . .
and choosing books about animals or sports
from Mrs. Tovani's shelves.

And . . .
he was eager for his turn
as the weekly keeper of Matisse,
the class mouse.

Then one morning,
Mrs. Tovani announced
that it was time to begin cursive.

Her third graders clapped and cheered.

Yes!

"I already know some cursive," Claire bragged.

"Me too—my brother taught me a lot of the letters,"
said Mike Greenwood.

But there was a flutter in Sean's stomach.
*What if he couldn't learn
this new style of handwriting?*

Sean looked at the table near his desk
and saw Matisse taking a nap in his cage.
Mice *never* had to worry about writing in cursive.

Mrs. Tovani handed out writing notebooks and said:

"We'll be working toward writing our names
in a legible and elegant way. . . .
We'll learn how to form each letter of the alphabet,
and we'll do the lowercase letters first."

Then she added,
"I hope all of you will learn this third grade skill
so I can induct you into the John Hancock Club."

Instantly,
Room 121 began to buzz:

"A club!" Andy said to Lucia.

"What did Mrs. Tovani say?"
asked Camilla.

"We get to be in the John Hancock Club . . . ,"
said Irene.

"Who's John Hancock?" asked Ben.

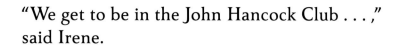

"What does 'induct' mean?"
Logan asked Julian.

"I *think* it means you're officially in
the club. . . ."

"Shhh . . . I can't hear . . . ,"
said Edward.

Mrs. Tovani waited to continue
until everyone was listening.
"I'll tell you more about our club in a few weeks,
but *first* we need to get to work
and learn how to write lowercase letters."

After that,
every morning during part of Language Arts,
Sean's class sharpened their pencils
and worked on the letters of the alphabet,
one at a time.

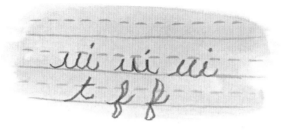

Mrs. Tovani stood at the blackboard
and showed her students how to loop letters,
and how to connect them to make words.

"Practice is the key," she said.

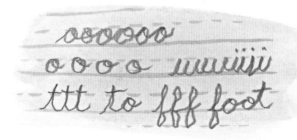

Sean always sat up straight and listened to his teacher.
Cursive writing seemed to have a language all its own . . .
with words like *ovals* and *understrokes* and *tails*.

"Your letters are almost A+!"
Mrs. Tovani said.
"I think we'll be able to write our names
by the end of November!"

One afternoon,
Mrs. Tovani gathered her students together and asked,
"What's your easiest letter?"
Right away, everyone had an answer.
"o!" "u!" "t!" "m!" "e!" "a!" "i!"

"What else can we say about cursive?" asked Mrs. Tovani.

"Once you get a letter right,
it's easier to do another one that has
the same tail or loop. . . ,"
said Lucia.

"Slanting my paper helps me,"
 said Mike.

Sean raised his hand.
"The *easy* part is that you start by learning just letters,
not words."

Edward chimed in.
"Yeah . . . just letters are easy!"

Ben said,
"Now that I know cursive,
I'll be able to read my mom's grocery list."

"Learning cursive is the best part about third grade!"
said Lindy.

The next week,
Mrs. Tovani held up a large poster.
At the top she had written the words

The John Hancock Club

in perfect script.
The rest of the poster was blank.

"After we learn our uppercase letters,
I'll be inducting members into this third grade club.
But . . . you have to earn the right to be a member
by showing me that you have *excellent* penmanship.

The new members will sign their names on this poster.
Then I'll hang it in the hallway so that everyone in the school
can see your beautiful handwriting."

Sean pictured the principal, Mr. Meeker;
his second grade teacher, Mrs. Foglietti;
and the rest of Hillside Elementary School
seeing the poster as they walked past Room 121.
He wanted to be sure that Sean McFerrin
was one of the names on the club member list.

By now,
Sean knew each lowercase letter.

Still,
he worried that he'd run into trouble writing his name.
Sean McFerrin had three uppercase letters,
and *F* looked especially tricky.

And *who* was John Hancock?

Sean and his classmates chattered about the club
on their way to Music and to Art.

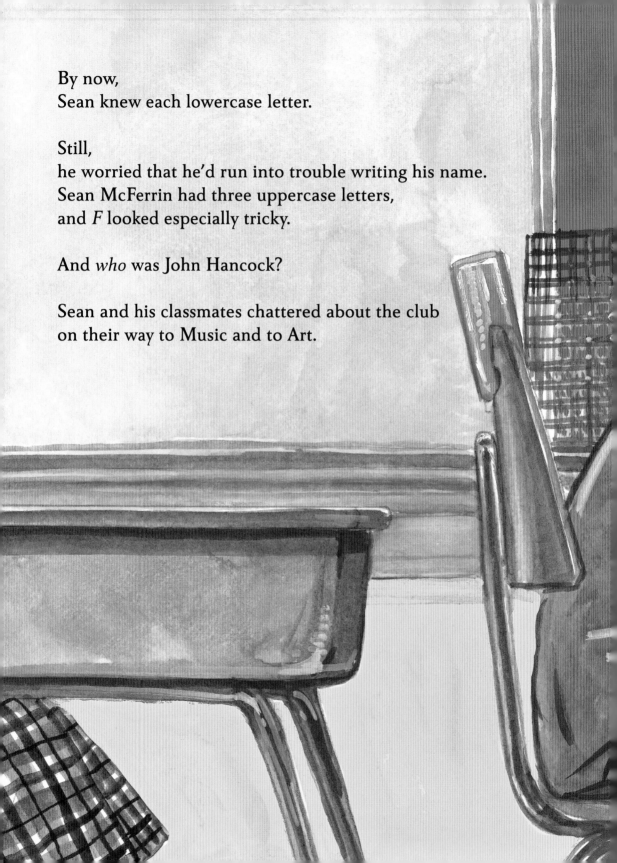

In November,
the third graders in Room 121
were busy learning other skills too.

Mrs. Tovani's lessons in math,
science,
reading,
and writing
blurred by . . .
and so did learning the uppercase cursive letters.

When the class wrote their favorite words
in their writing notebooks,
Sean tried to remember
his teacher's tips for good cursive:

*letter formation
uniformity
spacing
slant*

Sean worked on one tip at a time. . . .

hockey   recess   Saturday

Matisse   basketball

And Sean was still waiting for his turn
to take care of Matisse,
who ate his food and rustled in his cage
whenever he felt like it.

Finally, Mrs. Tovani told her class,
"Today we're going to learn *J* and *H* together
because they are important initials in Room 121."

Ben whispered to Sean, who whispered to Lindy:
"*J* is for John and *H* is for Hancock!"

After the lesson,
Mrs. Tovani held up an old-fashioned quill pen
and a black inkwell
and placed them on her desk.

"I think it's time we learned something about John Hancock
if we're going to join his club.
Can anyone tell the class who he is?"

The Hillside third graders sat at their desks,
puzzling over John Hancock.
No one knew who he was.

Mrs. Tovani chose a biography from her nonfiction shelf
and read aloud about John Hancock.
Later that week in the school library,
Sean and his class looked up more information about J. H.
Soon *everyone* in Mrs. Tovani's class
was a fan of Mr. John Hancock.

The third graders drew pictures of John Hancock
and taped them on a class mural in the hall.

Then they wrote sentences in cursive about parts of his life
and shared them with Mr. Meeker,
who stopped by their classroom for a surprise visit,
wearing a tricorner hat.

Lindy said:
"John Hancock
attended the Boston
Latin School . . . where
students had to work
on their penmanship
for *an hour* at the end
of each day."

Ellie said:
"John Hancock grew up to
be an important patriot in
the American Revolution. . . .
That's someone who wanted
America to be its own
country and not belong to
King George."

Camilla said:
"John Hancock
gave trees to his
town . . . and
fireworks for
celebrations."

Sean said:
"When John Hancock rode
through the streets of Boston
in his yellow carriage,
people cheered him
in an extraspecial way. . . .
They said,

Huzzah!

Huzzah!"

Sean loved saying
the funny new word
he'd learned from studying
about John Hancock.
And he liked writing
the double *z*'s.

When Mr. Meeker held up a copy
of the Declaration of Independence,
everyone noticed that John Hancock's signature
was the largest on the page.

It wasn't just big.

It was huge.

HUGE!

"Wow!" everyone said.
"It's twice as big as the other signatures!"

Now that Sean and his friends
knew about John Hancock's life
and his famous signature,
they couldn't wait to join his club.

During free time,
the students practiced writing their names.
Everyone wanted to make sure that their handwriting
was good enough to join the John Hancock Club.

Writing an *F* wasn't as tricky
as Sean had thought it would be,
and linking *rr* together was easy.
Double letters were like identical twins.

Sean smiled to himself when he looked at his name
at the top of his homework page.
Somehow *Sean McFerrin* looked more important
when he wrote it in ovals and loops.

The class felt like fourth graders
now that they could write their names
and spelling words
all in cursive:

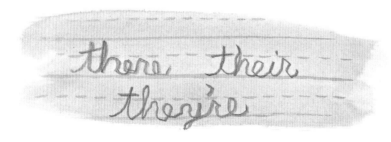

In fact,
no one wanted to write in plain old printing anymore.

One late November morning,
Mrs. Tovani announced to the class:

"It's high time we honor your hard work
and your beautiful penmanship.
Tomorrow I'll be inducting *everyone*
into the John Hancock Club . . .
and we'll have a party to celebrate."

There was a whir of commotion in Room 121.

"Yes!"
"We *all* made it!"
"Whew!"

Sean sat at his desk near Matisse's cage
with a big grin on his face.
Soon he would be a member
of the John Hancock Club!

Suddenly Sean had an idea.
And then *another* idea.

On the way to lunch that day,
he whispered his ideas to his teacher.
Mrs. Tovani nodded as she listened to Sean,
and then she quickly gave a note to Rose, the school cook,
when everyone passed through the cafeteria line.

The next day was one of the *very* best days of third grade.
It was the day that Mrs. Tovani
called off every name on her class list
to induct her students into the John Hancock Club.

First she taped a copy of J. H.'s famous signature
on the poster,
and then each third grader
dipped the feather pen into the inkwell
and signed his or her name
below John Hancock's . . .
using elegant cursive.

The quill sometimes dribbled a bit of ink,
and it was hard to sign the poster
in a perfectly straight line,
but nobody cared.

Writing with this special feather was an *honor* . . .
and John Hancock himself
had signed the Declaration of Independence
with a quill pen like this.

Mrs. Tovani introduced each new club member
to the rest of the class with an official flourish:

"Because of her excellence in cursive penmanship,
I present to Room 121
a new member of the John Hancock Club: *Lindy Brewer*!"

Then, after a signal from Mrs. Tovani,
Sean cheered for the new member
with just the right words,
and everyone else joined in:

"Huzzah! Huzzah!"

"Huzzah, huzzah!" "Huzzah, huzzah!"

"Huzzah, huzzah!"
"Huzzah! Huzzah!"

When it was Sean's turn,
he dipped the quill into the inkwell
and proudly signed his name.
His signature wasn't as huge as John Hancock's . . .
but the letters *S* and *M* and *F*
were all quite beautiful.

And so was the surprise treat
that Rose carried into Room 121
for the third graders' party.
Mr. Meeker showed up again in his tricorner hat . . .
just in time to watch Rose light the sparklers
that decorated a big cake.

After all,
John Hancock *did* like fireworks
at his celebrations.

Room 121 Epilogue

On a Monday in January,
Sean finally began his week
as keeper of the class mouse.

That day,
he hung a cardboard sign over Matisse's cage
for everyone in Room 121 to read.

H. Matisse

I share a name with the famous, French artist Henri Matisse who lived over a hundred years ago. Matisse became famous because he didn't paint his pictures in the plain old style. Instead, he used his colors in a new way to make his art more beautiful.

Mrs. Tovani told Sean
that the *H* and the *M* were the best she had seen yet,
and that the two *s*'s looked just like twins.

On Friday,
Mrs. Tovani added one more name
to the class list . . .
and with Sean's help,
Matisse was the very first mouse
inducted into the John Hancock Club.

The John Hancock Club

John Hancock

Ben Agresta

Edward J. Ayars

Claire Boswell

Lindy Brewer

Camilla Cornell

Marla Dolan

Teresa DeGood

Lily Flynn

Mike Greenwood

Den Hunter

Irene Hasenberg

George Koehler

Sean McFerrin

Paco Moore

Julian Muller

Andy Nagy

Ellie Paulsen

Lucia Bella Perez

Polly Rea

Will Secker

Cynthia Walker

John Windschill

H. Matisse

Margaret K. McElderry Books • An imprint of Simon & Schuster Children's Publishing Division • 1230 Avenue of the Americas, New York, New York 10020 • Text copyright © 2007 by Louise Borden • Illustrations copyright © 2007 by Adam Gustavson • All rights reserved, including the right of reproduction in whole or in part in any form. • Book design by Sonia Chaghatzbanian • The text for this book is set in Carre Noir. • The illustrations for this book are rendered in watercolors. Manufactured in China • 10 9 8 7 6 5 4 3 2 1 • Library of Congress Cataloging-in-Publication Data • Borden, Louise. The John Hancock Club / Louise Borden ; illustrated by Adam Gustavson.—1st ed. • p. cm. • Summary: Third grader Sean McFerrin wants to be part of the good penmanship club, but it all depends on how well he learns the new cursive writing. ISBN-13: 978-1-4169-1813-4 • ISBN-10: 1-4169-1813-2 (hardcover) • [1. Penmanship—Fiction. 2. Schools— Fiction. 3. Clubs—Fiction.] I. Gustavson, Adam, ill. II. Title. • PZ7.B64829Jo 2007 • [E]—dc22 • 2005033171

FIRST EDITION

Aa Bb Cc

Gg Hh Ii

Mm Nn Oo

Ss Tt Uu

Yy Zz